AN

INQUIRY

INTO

THE CAUSES AND EFFECTS

OF

THE VARIOLÆ VACCINÆ.

PRICE 7S. 6d.

AN

INQUIRY

INTO

THE CAUSES AND EFFECTS

OF

THE VARIOLÆ VACCINÆ,

A 'DISEASE

DISCOVERED IN SOME OF THE WESTERN COUNTIES OF ENGLAND,

PARTICULARLY

GLOUCESTERSHIRE,

AND KNOWN BY THE NAME OF

THE COW POX.

BY EDWARD JENNER, M.D. F.R.S. &c.

——— QUID NOBIS CERTIUS IPSIS
SENSIBUS ESSE POTEST, QUO VERA AC FALSA NOTEMUS.

LUCRETIUS.

London:

PRINTED, FOR THE AUTHOR,

BY SAMPSON LOW, N°. 7, BERWICK STREET, SOHO:

AND SOLD BY LAW, AVE-MARIA LANE; AND MURRAY AND HIGHLEY, FLEET STREET.

1798.

C. H PARRY, M. D.

AT BATH.

MY DEAR FRIEND,

IN the prefent age of fcientific inveftigation, it is remarkable that a difeafe of fo peculiar a nature as the Cow Pox, which has appeared in this and fome of the neighbouring counties for fuch a feries of years, fhould fo long have efcaped particular attention. Finding the prevailing notions on the fubject, both among men of our profeffion and others, extremely vague and indeterminate, and conceiving that facts might ap-

pear

pear at once both curious and useful, I have insti-
tuted as strict an inquiry into the causes and effects
of this singular malady as local circumstances would
admit.

The following pages are the result, which, from
motives of the most affectionate regard, are dedi-
cated to you, by

Your sincere Friend,

EDWARD JENNER.

Berkeley, Gloucestershire,
    June 21st, 1798.

INQUIRY,

&c. &c.

THE deviation of Man from the ſtate in which he was originally placed by Nature ſeems to have proved to him a prolific ſource of Diſeaſes. From the love of ſplendour, from the indulgences of luxury, and from his fondneſs for amuſement, he has familiariſed himſelf with a great number of animals, which may not originally have been intended for his aſſociates.

The

The Wolf, difarmed of ferocity, is now pillowed in the lady's lap*. The Cat, the little Tyger of our ifland, whofe natural home is the foreft, is equally domefticated and careffed. The Cow, the Hog, the Sheep, and the Horfe, are all, for a variety of purpofes, brought under his care and dominion.

There is a difeafe to which the Horfe, from his ftate of domeftication, is frequently fubject. The Farriers have termed it *the Greafe*. It is an inflammation and fwelling in the heel, from which iffues matter poffeffing properties of a very peculiar kind, which feems capable of generating a difeafe in the Human Body (after it has undergone the modification which I fhall prefently fpeak of), which bears fo ftrong a refemblance to the Small Pox, that I think it highly probable it may be the fource of that difeafe.

* The late Mr. John Hunter proved, by experiments, that the Dog is the Wolf in a degenerated ftate.

In

In this Dairy Country a great number of Cows are kept, and the office of milking is performed indiscriminately by Men and Maid Servants. One of the former having been appointed to apply dreffings to the heels of a Horfe affected with *the Greafe*, and not paying due attention to cleanli-nefs, incautiously bears his part in milking the Cows, with fome particles of the infectious matter adhering to his fingers. When this is the cafe, it commonly happens that a difeafe is communicated to the Cows, and from the Cows to the Dairy-maids, which fpreads through the farm until moft of the cattle and domeftics feel its unpleafant confequences. This difeafe has obtained the name of the Cow Pox. It appears on the nipples of the Cows in the form of irregular puftules. At their firft appearance they are commonly of a palifh blue, or rather of a colour fomewhat approaching to livid, and are furrounded by an eryfipelatous in-

flammation.

flammation. Thefe puftules, unlefs a timely remedy be applied, frequently degenerate into phagedenic ulcers, which prove extremely troublefome *. The animals become indifpofed, and the
fecretion of milk is much leffened. Inflamed fpots
now begin to appear on different parts of the hands
of the domeftics employed in milking, and fometimes on the wrifts, which quickly run on to fup-
puration, firft affuming the appearance of the fmall
vefications produced by a burn. Moft commonly
they appear about the joints of the fingers, and
at their extremities; but whatever parts are af-
ected, if the fituation will admit, thefe fuperficial
fuppurations put on a circular form, with their
edges more elevated than their centre, and of a

---

* They who attend fick cattle in this country find a fpeedy remedy for ftopping
the progrefs of this complaint in thofe applications which act chemically upon
the morbid matter, fuch as the folutions of the Vitriolum Zinci, the Vitriolum
Cupri, &c.

colour

colour diftantly approaching to blue. Abforption takes place, and tumours appear in each axilla. The fyftem becomes affected — the pulfe is quickened; and fhiverings, with general laffitude and pains about the loins and limbs, with vomiting, come on. The head is painful, and the patient is now and then even affected with delirium. Thefe fymptoms, varying in their degrees of violence, generally continue from one day to three or four, leaving ulcerated fores about the hands, which, from the fenfibility of the parts, are very troublefome, and commonly heal flowly, frequently becoming phagedenic, like thofe from whence they fprung. The lips, noftrils, eyelids, and other parts of the body, are fometimes affected with fores; but thefe evidently arife from their being needlefsly rubbed or fcratched with the patient's infected fingers. No eruptions on the fkin have followed the decline of the feverifh fymptoms in any inftance that has

come

come under my infpection, one only excepted, and in this cafe a very few appeared on the arms : they were very minute, of a vivid red colour, and foon died away without advancing to maturation; fo that I cannot determine whether they had any connection with the preceding fymptoms.

Thus the difeafe makes its progrefs from the Horfe to the nipple of the Cow, and from the Cow to the Human Subject.

Morbid matter of various kinds, when abforbed into the fyftem, may produce effects in fome degree fimilar; but what renders the Cow-pox virus fo extremely fingular, is, that the perfon who has been thus affected is for ever after fecure from the infection of the Small Pox; neither expofure to the variolous effluvia, nor the infertion of the matter into the fkin, producing this diftemper.

In

In fupport of fo extraordinary a fact, I fhall lay before my Reader a great number of inftances *.

* It is neceffary to obferve, that puftulous fores frequently appear fpontaneoufly on the nipples of Cows, and inftances have occurred, though very rarely, of the hands of the fervants employed in milking being affected with fores in confequence, and even of their feeling an indifpofition from abforption. Thefe puftules are of a much milder nature than thofe which arife from that contagion which conftitutes the true Cow Pox. They are always free from the bluifh or livid tint fo confpicuous in the puftules in that difeafe. No eryfipelas attends them, nor do they fhew any phagedenic difpofition as in the other cafe, but quickly terminate in a fcab without creating any apparent diforder in the Cow. This complaint appears at various feafons of the year, but moft commonly in the Spring, when the Cows are firft taken from their winter food and fed with grafs. It is very apt to appear alfo when they are fuckling their young. But this difeafe is not be confidered as fimilar in any refpect to that of which I am treating, as it is incapable of producing any fpecific effects on the human Conftitution. However, it is of the greateft confequence to point it out here, left the want of difcrimination fhould occafion an idea of fecurity from the infection of the Small Pox, which might prove delufive.

CASE

CASE I.

JOSEPH MERRET, now an Under Gardener to the Earl of Berkeley, lived as a Servant with a Farmer near this place in the year 1770, and occafionally affifted in milking his mafter's cows. Several horfes belonging to the farm began to have fore heels, which Merret frequently attended. The cows foon became affected with the Cow Pox, and foon after feveral fores appeared on his hands. Swellings and ftiffnefs in each axilla followed, and he was fo much indifpofed for feveral days as to be incapable of purfuing his ordinary employment. Previoufly to the appearance of the diftemper among the cows there was no frefh cow brought into the farm, nor any fervant employed who was affected with the Cow Pox.

In April, 1795, a general inoculation taking place here, Merret was inoculated with his family; fo that a period of twenty-five years had elapfed from his having the Cow Pox

C

to this time. However, though the variolous matter was repeatedly inferted into his arm, I found it impracticable to infect him with it; an efflorefcence only, taking on an eryfipelatous look about the centre, appearing on the fkin near the punctured parts. During the whole time that his family had the Small Pox, one of whom had it very full, he remained in the houfe with them, but received no injury from expofure to the contagion.

It is neceffary to obferve, that the utmoft care was taken to afcertain, with the moft fcrupulous precifion, that no one whofe cafe is here adduced had gone through the Small Pox previous to thefe attempts to produce that difeafe.

Had thefe experiments been conducted in a large city, or in a populous neighbourhood, fome doubts might have been entertained; but here, where population is thin, and where fuch an event as a perfon's having had the Small Pox is always faithfully recorded, no rifk of inaccuracy in this particular can arife.

CASE

CASE II.

SARAH PORTLOCK, of this place, was infected with the Cow Pox, when a Servant at a Farmer's in the neighbourhood, twenty-feven years ago *.

In the year 1792, conceiving herfelf, from this circumftance, fecure from the infection of the Small Pox, fhe nurfed one of her own children who had accidentally caught the difeafe, but no indifpofition enfued.—During the time fhe remained in the infected room, variolous matter was inferted into both her arms, but without any further effect than in the preceding cafe.

* I have purpofely felected feveral cafes in which the difeafe had appeared at a very diftant period previous to the experiments made with variolous matter, to fhew that the change produced in the conftitution is not affected by time.

 CASE

CASE III.

JOHN PHILLIPS, a Tradeſman of this town, had the Cow Pox at ſo early a period as nine years of age. At the age of ſixty-two I inoculated him, and was very careful in ſelecting matter in its moſt active ſtate. It was taken from the arm of a boy juſt before the commencement of the eruptive fever, and inſtantly inſerted. It very ſpeedily produced a ſting-like feel in the part. An effloreſcence appeared, which on the fourth day was rather extenſive, and ſome degree of pain and ſtiffneſs were felt about the ſhoulder; but on the fifth day theſe ſymptoms began to diſappear, and in a day or two after went entirely off, without producing any effect on the ſyſtem.

CASE

CASE IV.

MARY BARGE, of Woodford, in this parifh, was inoculated with variolous matter in the year 1791. An efflorefcence of a palifh red colour foon appeared about the
parts where the matter was inferted, and fpread itfelf rather
extenfively, but died away in a few days without producing
any variolous fymptoms *. She has fince been repeatedly
employed as a nurfe to Small-pox patients, without expe-
riencing any ill confequences. This woman had the Cow
Pox when fhe lived in the fervice of a Farmer in this parifh
thirty-one years before.

---

* It is remarkable that variolous matter, when the fyftem is difpofed to rejeĉt
it, fhould excite inflammation on the part to which it is applied more fpeedily
than when it produces the Small Pox. Indeed it becomes almoft a criterion by
which we can determine whether the infeĉtion will be received or not. It feems
as if a change, which endures through life, had been produced in the aĉtion, or
difpofition to aĉtion, in the veffels of the fkin; and it is remarkable too, that
whether this change has been effeĉted by the Small Pox, or the Cow Pox, that
the difpofition to fudden cuticular inflammation is the fame on the application of
variolous matter.

CASE

CASE V.

MRS. H——, a respectable Gentlewoman of this town, had the Cow Pox when very young. She received the infection in rather an uncommon manner: it was given by means of her handling some of the same utensils * which were in use among the servants of the family, who had the disease from milking infected cows. Her hands had many of the Cow-pox sores upon them, and they were communicated to her nose, which became inflamed and very much swoln. Soon after this event Mrs. H—— was exposed to the contagion of the Small Pox, where it was scarcely possible for her to have escaped, had she been susceptible of it, as she regularly attended a relative who had the disease in so violent a degree that it proved fatal to him.

---

* When the Cow Pox has prevailed in the dairy, it has often been communicated to those who have not milked the cows, by the handle of the milk pail.

In

In the year 1778 the Small Pox prevailed very much at Berkeley, and Mrs. H—— not feeling perfectly fatisfied refpecting her fafety (no indifpofition having followed her expofure to the Small Pox) I inoculated her with active variolous matter   The fame appearance followed as in the preceding cafes — an efflorefcence on the arm without any effect on the conftitution.

CASE VI.

IT is a fact fo well known among our Dairy Farmers, that thofe who have had the Small Pox either efcape the Cow Pox or are difpofed to have it flightly; that as foon as the complaint fhews itfelf among the cattle, affiftants are procured, if poffible, who are thus rendered lefs fufceptible of it, otherwife the bufinefs of the farm could fcarcely go forward.

In the month of May, 1796, the Cow Pox broke out at Mr. Baker's, a Farmer who lives near this place.   The
                                                        difeafe

difeafe was communicated by means of a cow which was purchafed in an infected ftate at a neighbouring fair, and not one of the Farmer's cows (confifting of thirty) which were at that time milked efcaped the contagion. The family confifted of a man fervant, two dairymaids, and a fervant boy, who, with the Farmer himfelf, were twice a day employed in milking the cattle. The whole of this family, except Sarah Wynne, one of the dairymaids, had gone through the Small Pox. The confequence was, that the Farmer and the fervant boy efcaped the infection of the Cow Pox entirely, and the fervant man and one of the maid fervants had each of them nothing more than a fore on one of their fingers, which produced no diforder in the fyftem. But the other dairymaid, Sarah Wynne, who never had the Small Pox, did not efcape in fo eafy a manner. She caught the complaint from the cows, and was affected with the fymptoms defcribed in the 5th page in fo violent a degree, that fhe was confined to her bed, and rendered incapable for feveral days of purfuing her ordinary vocations in the farm.

March

March 28th, 1797, I inoculated this girl, and carefully rubbed the variolous matter into two flight incifions made upon the left arm. A little inflammation appeared in the ufual manner around the parts where the matter was inferted, but fo early as the fifth day it vanifhed entirely without producing any effect on the fyftem.

CASE VII.

ALTHOUGH the preceding hiftory pretty clearly evinces that the conftitution is far lefs fufceptible of the contagion of the Cow Pox after it has felt that of the Small Pox, and although in general, as I have obferved, they who have had the Small Pox, and are employed in milking cows which are infected with the Cow Pox, either efcape the diforder, or have fores on the hands without feeling any general indifpofition, yet the animal economy is fubject to fome variation in this refpect, which the following relation will point out:

D   In

In the fummer of the year 1796 the Cow Pox appeared at the Farm of Mr. Andrews, a confiderable dairy adjoining to the town of Berkeley. It was communicated, as in the preceding inftance, by an infected cow purchafed at a fair in the neighbourhood. The family confifted of the Farmer, his wife, two fons, a man and a maid fervant; all of whom, except the Farmer (who was fearful of the confequences), bore a part in milking the cows. The whole of them, exclufive of the man fervant, had regularly gone through the Small Pox; but in this cafe no one who milked the cows efcaped the contagion. All of them had fores upon their hands, and fome degree of general indifpofition, preceded by pains and tumours in the axillæ: but there was no comparifon in the feverity of the difeafe as it was felt by the fervant man, who had efcaped the Small Pox, and by thofe of the family who had not, for, while he was confined to his bed, they were able, without much inconvenience, to follow their ordinary bufinefs.

February

February the 13th, 1797, I availed myfelf of an opportunity of inoculating William Rodway, the fervant man above alluded to. Variolous matter was inferted into both his arms; in the right by means of fuperficial incifions, and into the left by flight punctures into the cutis. Both were perceptibly inflamed on the third day. After this the inflammation about the punctures foon died away, but a fmall appearance of eryfipelas was manifeft about the edges of the incifions till the eighth day, when a little uneafinefs was felt for the fpace of half an hour in the right axilla. The inflammation then haftily difappeared without producing the moft diftant mark of affection of the fyftem.

D 2   *CASE*

CASE VIII.

ELIZABETH WYNNE, aged fifty-feven, lived as a fervant with a neighbouring Farmer thirty-eight years ago. She was then a dairymaid, and the Cow Pox broke out among the cows. She caught the difeafe with the reft of the family, but, compared with them, had it in a very flight degree, one very fmall fore only breaking out on the little finger of her left hand, and fcarcely any perceptible indifpofition following it.

As the malady had fhewn itfelf in fo flight a manner, and as it had taken place at fo diftant a period of her life, I was happy with the opportunity of trying the effects of variolous matter upon her conftitution, and on the 28th of March, 1797, I inoculated her by making two fuperficial incifions on the left arm, on which the matter was cautioufly rubbed. A little efflorefcence foon appeared, and a tin-

gling

gling fenfation was felt about the parts where the matter was inferted until the third day, when both began to fubfide, and fo early as the fifth day it was evident that no indifpofition would follow.

CASE IX.

ALTHOUGH the Cow Pox fhields the conftitution from the Small Pox, and the Small Pox proves a protection againft its own future poifon, yet it appears that the human body is again and again fufceptible of the infectious matter of the Cow Pox, as the following hiftory will demonftrate:

William Smith, of Pyrton in this parifh, contracted this difeafe when he lived with a neighbouring Farmer in the year 1780. One of the horfes belonging to the farm had fore heels, and it fell to his lot to attend him. By thefe means the infection was carried to the cows, and from the cows it was communicated to Smith. On one of his hands were

were feveral ulcerated fores, and he was affected with fuch fymptoms as have been before defcribed.

In the year 1791 the Cow Pox broke out at another farm where he then lived as a fervant, and he became affected with it a fecond time; and in the year 1794 he was fo unfortunate as to catch it again. The difeafe was equally as fevere the fecond and third time as it was on the firft *.

In the fpring of the year 1795 he was twice inoculated, but no affection of the fyftem could be produced from the variolous matter; and he has fince affociated with thofe who had the Small Pox in its moft contagious ftate without feeling any effect from it.

* This is not the cafe in general — a fecond attack is commonly very flight, and fo, I am informed, it is among the cows.

CASE

CASE X.

SIMON NICHOLS lived as a fervant with Mr. Brom-edge, a gentleman who refides on his own farm in this parifh, in the year 1782. He was employed in applying dreffings to the fore heels of one of his mafter's horfes, and at the fame time affifted in milking the cows. The cows became affected in confequence, but the difeafe did not fhew itfelf on their nipples till feveral weeks after he had begun to drefs the horfe. He quitted Mr. Bromedge's fervice, and went to another farm without any fores upon him; but here his hands foon began to be affected in the common way, and he was much indifpofed with the ufual fymptoms. Concealing the nature of the malady from Mr. Cole, his new mafter, and being there alfo employed in milking, the Cow Pox was communicated to the cows.

Some

Some years afterwards Nichols was employed in a farm where the Small Pox broke out, when I inoculated him with feveral other patients, with whom he continued during the whole time of their confinement. His arm inflamed, but neither the inflammation nor his affociating with the inoculated family produced the leaft effect upon his conftitution.

CASE XI.

WILLIAM STINCHCOMB was a fellow fervant with Nichols at Mr. Bromedge's Farm at the time the cattle had the Cow Pox, and he was unfortunately infected by them. His left hand was very feverely affected with feveral corroding ulcers, and a tumour of confiderable fize appeared in the axilla of that fide. His right hand had only one fmall fore upon it, and no fore difcovered itfelf in the correfponding axilla.

In

In the year 1792 Stinchcomb was inoculated with variolous matter, but no confequences enfued beyond a little inflammation in the arm for a few days. A large party were inoculated at the fame time, fome of whom had the difeafe in a more violent degree than is commonly feen from inoculation. He purpofely affociated with them, but could not receive the Small Pox.

During the fickening of fome of his companions, their fymptoms fo ftrongly recalled to his mind his own ftate when fickening with the Cow Pox, that he very pertinently remarked their ftriking fimilarity.

E   *CASE*

CASE XII.

THE Paupers of the village of Tortworth, in this county, were inoculated by Mr. Henry Jenner, Surgeon, of Berkeley, in the year 1795. Among them, eight patients prefented themfelves who had at different periods of their lives had the Cow Pox. One of them, Hefter Walkley, I attended with that difeafe when fhe lived in the fervice of a Farmer in the fame village in the year 1782; but neither this woman, nor any other of the patients who had gone through the Cow Pox, received the variolous infection either from the arm or from mixing in the fociety of the other patients who were inoculated at the fame time. This ftate of fecurity proved a fortunate circumftance, as many of the poor women were at the fame time in a ftate of pregnancy.

CASE

CASE XIII.

One inſtance has occurred to me of the ſyſtem being affected from the matter iſſuing from the heels of horſes, and of its remaining afterwards unſuſceptible of the variolous contagion; another, where the Small Pox appeared obſcurely; and a third, in which its complete exiſtence was poſitively aſcertained.

Firſt, THOMAS PEARCE, is the ſon of a Smith and Farrier near to this place. He never had the Cow Pox; but, in conſequence of dreſſing horſes with ſore heels at his father's, when a lad, he had ſores on his fingers which ſuppurated, and which occaſioned a pretty ſevere indiſpoſition. Six years afterwards I inſerted variolous matter into his arm repeatedly, without being able to produce any thing more than ſlight inflammation, which appeared very ſoon

E 2

after

after the matter was applied, and afterwards I expofed him to the contagion of the Small Pox with as little effect *.

CASE XIV.

Secondly, Mr. JAMES COLE, a Farmer in this parifh, had a difeafe from the fame fource as related in the preceding cafe, and fome years after was inoculated with variolous matter. He had a little pain in the axilla, and felt a flight indifpofition for three or four hours. A few eruptions fhewed themfelves on the forehead, but they very foon difappeared without advancing to maturation.

---

* It is a remarkable fact, and well known to many, that we are frequently foiled in our endeavours to communicate the Small Pox by inoculation to blackfmiths, who in the country are farriers. They often, as in the above inftance, either refift the contagion entirely, or have the difeafe anomaloufly. Shall we not be able now to account for this on a rational principle?

CASE

CASE XV.

Although in the two former inftances the fyftem feemed to be fecured, or nearly fo, from variolous infection, by the abforption of matter from fores produced by the difeafed heels of horfes, yet the following cafe decifively proves that this cannot be entirely relied upon, until a difeafe has been generated by the morbid matter from the horfe on the nipple of the cow, and paffed through that medium to the human fubject.

Mr. ABRAHAM RIDDIFORD, a Farmer at Stone in this parifh, in confequence of dreffing a mare that had fore heels, was affected with very painful fores in both his hands, tumours in each axilla, and fevere and general indifpofition. A Surgeon in the neighbourhood attended him, who, knowing the fimilarity between the appearance of the fores upon his hands and thofe produced by the

Cow

Cow Pox, and being acquainted alfo with the effects of that difeafe on the human conftitution, affured him that he never need to fear the infection of the Small Pox; but this affertion proved fallacious, for, on being expofed to the infection upwards of twenty years afterwards, he caught the difeafe, which took its regular courfe in a very mild way. There certainly was a difference perceptible, although it is not eafy to defcribe it, in the general appearance of the puftules from that which we commonly fee. Other practitioners, who vifited the patient at my requeft, agreed with me in this point, though there was no room left for fufpicion as to the reality of the difeafe, as I inoculated fome of his family from the puftules, who had the Small Pox, with its ufual appearances, in confequence.

CASE

CASE XVI.

SARAH NELMES, a dairymaid at a Farmer's near this place, was infected with the Cow Pox from her master's cows in May, 1796. She received the infection on a part of the hand which had been previously in a slight degree injured by a scratch from a thorn. A large pustulous sore and the usual symptoms accompanying the disease were produced in consequence. The pustule was so expressive of the true character of the Cow Pox, as it commonly appears upon the hand, that I have given a representation of it in the annexed plate. The two small pustules on the wrists arose also from the application of the virus to some minute abrasions of the cuticle, but the livid tint, if they ever had any, was not conspicuous at the time I saw the patient. The pustule on the fore finger shews the disease in an earlier stage. It did not actually appear on the hand of

this

this young woman, but was taken from that of another, and is annexed for the purpofe of reprefenting the malady after it has newly appeared.

CASE XVII.

THE more accurately to obferve the progrefs of the infection, I felected a healthy boy, about eight years old, for the purpofe of inoculation for the Cow Pox. The matter was taken from a fore on the hand of a dairymaid *, who was infected by her mafter's cows, and it was inferted, on the 14th of May, 1796, into the arm of the boy by means of two fuperficial incifions, barely penetrating the cutis, each about half an inch long.

* From the fore on the hand of Sarah Nelmes. — See the preceding cafe and the plate.

On

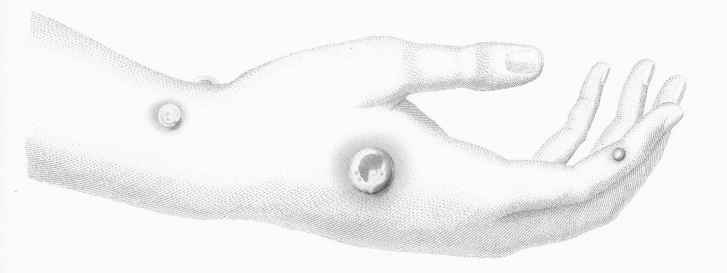

W. Skelton del.ᵗ et sculp.ᵗ

On the feventh day he complained of uneafinefs in the axilla, and on the ninth he became a little chilly, loft his appetite, and had a flight head-ach. During the whole of this day he was perceptibly indifpofed, and fpent the night with fome degree of reftleffnefs, but on the day following he was perfectly well.

The appearance of the incifions in their progrefs to a ftate of maturation were much the fame as when produced in a fimilar manner by variolous matter. The only difference which I perceived was, in the ftate of the limpid fluid arifing from the action of the virus, which affumed rather a darker hue, and in that of the efflorefcence fpreading round the incifions, which had more of an eryfipelatous look than we commonly perceive when variolous matter has been made ufe of in the fame manner; but the whole died away (leaving on the inoculated parts fcabs and fubfequent efchars) without giving me or my patient the leaft trouble.

F In

In order to afcertain whether the boy, after feeling fo flight an affection of the fyftem from the Cow-pox virus, was fecure from the contagion of the Small-pox, he was inoculated the 1ft of July following with variolous matter, immediately taken from a puftule. Several flight punctures and incifions were made on both his arms, and the matter was carefully inferted, but no difeafe followed. The fame appearances were obfervable on the arms as we commonly fee when a patient has had variolous matter applied, after having either the Cow-pox or the Small-pox. Several months afterwards, he was again inoculated with variolous matter, but no fenfible effect was produced on the conftitution.

Here my refearches were interrupted till the fpring of the year 1798, when from the wetnefs of the early part of the feafon, many of the farmers' horfes in this neighbourhood were affected with fore heels, in confequence of which the Cow-pox broke out among feveral of our dairies, which afforded me an opportunity of making further obfervations upon this curious difeafe.

A mare,

A mare, the property of a perfon who keeps a dairy in a neighbouring parifh, began to have fore heels the latter end of the month of February 1798, which were occafionally wafhed by the fervant men of the farm, Thomas Virgoe, William Wherret, and William Haynes, who in confequence became affected with fores in their hands, followed by inflamed lymphatic glands in the arms and axillæ, fhiverings fucceeded by heat, laffitude and general pains in the limbs. A fingle paroxyfm terminated the difeafe; for within twenty-four hours they were free from general indifpofition, nothing remaining but the fores on their hands. Haynes and Virgoe, who had gone through the Small-pox from inoculation, defcribed their feelings as very fimilar to thofe which affected them on fickening with that malady. Wherret never had had the Small-pox. Haynes was daily employed as one of the milkers at the farm, and the difeafe began to fhew itfelf among the cows about ten days after he firft affifted in wafhing the mare's heels. Their nipples became fore in the ufual way, with blueifh puftules; but as remedies were early applied they did not ulcerate to any extent.

CASE

CASE XVIII.

JOHN BAKER, a child of five years old, was inoculated March 16, 1798, with matter taken from a puſtule on the hand of Thomas Virgoe, one of the ſervants who had been infeſted from the mare's heels. He became ill on the 6th day with ſymptoms ſimilar to thoſe excited by Cow-pox matter. On the 8th day he was free from indiſpoſition.

There was ſome variation in the appearance of the puſtule on the arm. Although it ſomewhat reſembled a Small-pox puſtule, yet its ſimilitude was not ſo conſpicuous as when excited by matter from the nipple of the cow, or when the matter has paſſed from thence through the medium of the human ſubjeſt.—(See Plate, No. 2.)

This experiment was made to aſcertain the progreſs and ſubſequent effeſts of the diſeaſe when thus propagated.

We

Edw.d Pearce del.t

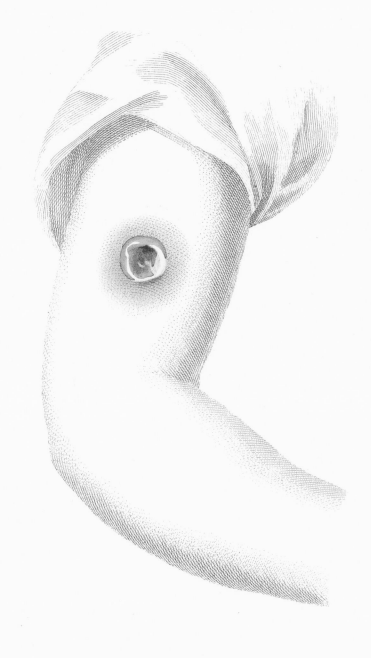

Will.m Skelton sculp.t

We have feen that the virus from the horfe, when it proves infectious to the human fubject is not to be relied upon as rendering the fyftem fecure from variolous infection, but that the matter produced by it upon the nipple of the cow is perfectly fo. Whether its paffing from the horfe through the human conftitution, as in the prefent inftance, will produce a fimilar effect, remains to be decided. This would now have been effected, but the boy was rendered unfit for inoculation from having felt the effects of a contagious fever in a work-houfe, foon after this experiment was made.

CASE XIX.

WILLIAM SUMMERS, a child of five years and a half old was inoculated the fame day with Baker, with matter taken from the nipples of one of the infected cows, at the farm alluded to in page 35. He became indifpofed on the 6th day, vomited once, and felt the ufual flight fymptoms till the 8th day, when he appeared perfectly well. The progrefs of the puftule, formed by the infection of the virus

was

was fimilar to that noticed in Cafe XVII., with this exception, its being free from the livid tint obferved in that inftance.

CASE XX.

FROM William Summers the difeafe was transfered to William Pead a boy of eight years old, who was inoculated March 28th. On the 6th day he complained of pain in the axilla, and on the 7th was affected with the common fymptoms of a patient fickening with the Small-pox from inoculation, which did not terminate 'till the 3d day after the feizure. So perfect was the fimilarity to the variolous fever that I was induced to examine the fkin, conceiving there might have been fome eruptions, but none appeared. The efflorefcent blufh around the part punctured in the boy's arm was fo truly characteriftic of that which appears on variolous inoculation, that I have given a reprefentation of it. The drawing was made when the puftule was begining to die away, and the areola retiring from the centre. (See Plate, No. 3.)

CASE

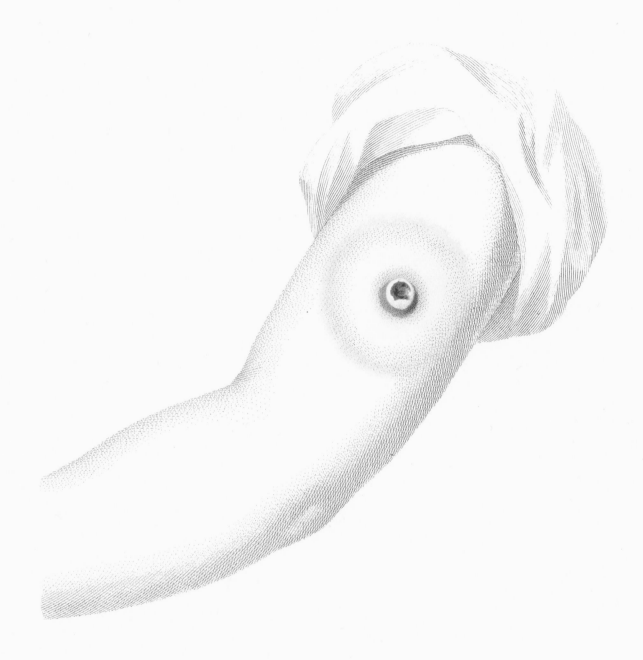

Edw.ᵈ Pearce del.ᵗ

Will.ᵐ Skelton sculp

CASE XXI.

APRIL 5th.   Several children and adults were inoculated from the arm of William Pead. The greater part of them fickened on the 6th day, and were well on the 7th, but in three of the number a fecondary indifpofition arofe in confequence of an extenfive eryfipelatous inflammation which appeared on the inoculated arms. It feemed to arife from the ftate of the puftule, which fpread out, accompanied with fome degree of pain, to about half the diameter of a fix-pence.   One of thefe patients was an infant of half a year old.   By the application of mercurial ointment to the inflamed parts (a treatment recommended under fimilar circumftances in the inoculated Small-pox) the complaint fubfided without giving much trouble.

HANNAH EXCELL an healthy girl of feven years old, and one of the patients above mentioned, received the
infection

infection from the infertion of the virus under the cuticle of the arm in three diftinct points. The puftules which arofe in confequence, fo much refembled, on the 12th day, thofe appearing from the infertion of variolous matter, that an experienced Inoculator would fcarcely have difcovered a fhade of difference at that period. Experience now tells me that almoft the only variation which follows confifts in the puftulous fluids remaining limpid nearly to the time of its total difappearance; and not, as in the direct Small-pox, becoming purulent.—(See Plate, No. 4.)

CASE XXII.

FROM the arm of this girl matter was taken and inferted April 12th into the arms of John Macklove one year and a half old,

Robert F. Jenner, eleven months old,

Mary Pead, 5 years old, and

Mary James, 6 years old.

Among

Edw.ᵈ Pearce del.ᵗ

Will.ᵐ Skelton sculp.ᵗ

Among thefe Robert F. Jenner did not receive the infection. The arms of the other three inflamed properly and
began to affect the fyftem in the ufual manner; but being
under fome apprehenfions from the preceding Cafes that a
troublefome eryfipelas might arife, I determined on making
an experiment with the view of cutting off its fource.
Accordingly after the patients had felt an indifpofition of
about twelve hours, I applied in two of thefe Cafes out of
the three, on the veficle formed by the virus, a little mild
cauftic, compofed of equal parts of quick-lime and foap,
and fuffered it to remain on the part fix hours *. It feemed
to give the children but little uneafinefs, and effectually
anfwered my intention in preventing the appearance of
eryfipelas. Indeed it feemed to do more, for in half an
hour after its application, the indifpofition of the children
ceafed †. Thefe precautions were perhaps unneceffary as

* Perhaps a few touches with the lapis fcepticus would have proved equally
efficacious.

† What effect would a fimilar treatment produce in inoculation for the Small-
pox?

G   the

the arm of the third child, Mary Pead, which was suffered
to take its common course, scabbed quickly, without any
eryfipelas.

CASE XXIII.

FROM this child's arm matter was taken and transferred
to that of J. Barge, a boy of seven years old. He sickened
on the 8th day, went through the disease with the usual
flight symptoms, and without any inflammation on the arm
beyond the common efflorefcence furrounding the puftule,
an appearance fo often feen in inoculated Small-pox.

After the many fruitlefs attempts to give the Small-pox to
thofe who had had the Cow-pox, it did not appear neceffary, nor was it convenient to me, to inoculate the whole of
thofe who had been the fubjects of thefe late trials; yet I
thought it right to fee the effects of variolous matter on
fome of them, particularly William Summers, the firft of
thefe patients who had been infected with matter taken

from

from the cow. He was therefore inoculated with variolous matter from a frefh puftule; but, as in the preceding Cafes, the fyftem did not feel the effects of it in the fmalleft degree. I had an opportunity alfo of having this boy and William Pead inoculated by my Nephew, Mr. Henry Jenner, whofe report to me is as follows: " I have inoculated Pead and Barge, two of the boys whom you lately infected with the Cow-pox. On the 2d day the incifions were in-flamed and there was a pale inflammatory ftain around them. On the 3d day thefe appearances were ftill increafing and their arms itched confiderably. On the 4th day, the inflammation was evidently fubfiding, and on the 6th it was fcarcely perceptible. No fymptom of indifpofition followed.

To convince myfelf that the variolous matter made ufe of was in a perfect ftate, I at the fame time inoculated a patient with fome of it who never had gone through the Cow-pox, and it produced the Small-pox in the ufual regular manner."

Thefe

Thefe experiments afforded me much fatisfaction, they proved that the matter in paffing from one human fubject to another, through five gradations, loft none of its original properties, J. Barge being the fifth who received the infection fucceffively from William Summers, the boy to whom it was communicated from the cow.

I fhall

I fhall now conclude this Inquiry with fome general obfervations on the fubject and on fome others which are interwoven with it.

Although I prefume it may be unneceffary to produce further teftimony in fupport of my affertion " that the Cow-pox protects the human conftitution from the infection of the Small-pox," yet it affords me confiderable fatisfaction to fay, that Lord Somerville, the Prefident of the Board of Agriculture, to whom this paper was fhewn by Sir Jofeph Banks, has found upon inquiry that the ftatements were confirmed by the concuring teftimony of Mr. Dolland, a furgeon, who refides in a dairy country remote from this, in which thefe obfervations were made. With refpect to the opinion adduced " that the fource of the infection

is

is a peculiar morbid matter arifing in the horfe,"
although I have not been able to prove it from
actual experiments conducted immediately under
my own eye, yet the evidence I have adduced
appears fufficient to eftablifh it.

They who are not in the habit of conducting
experiments may not be aware of the coincidence
of circumftances neceffary for their being managed
fo as to prove perfectly decifive; nor how often men
engaged in profeffional purfuits are liable to inter-
ruptions which difappoint them almoft at the
inftant of their being accomplifhed: however,
I feel no room for hefitation refpecting the common origin of the difeafe, being well convinced
that it never appears among the cows (except it
can be traced to a cow introduced among the
general

general herd which has been previoufly infected,
or to an infected fervant), unlefs they have been
milked by fome one who, at the fame time, has
the care of a horfe affected with difeafed heels.

The fpring of the year 1797, which I intended
particularly to have devoted to the completion of
this inveftigation, proved, from its drynefs, re-
markably adverfe to my wifhes; for it frequently
happens, while the farmers' horfes are expofed to
the cold rains which fall at that feafon that their
heels become difeafed, and no Cow-pox then
appeared in the neighbourhood.

The active quality of the virus from the horfes'
heels is greatly increafed after it has acted on the
nipples of the cow, as it rarely happens that the
horfe

horfe affects his dreffer with fores, and as rarely that a milk-maid efcapes the infection when fhe milks infected cows. It is moft active at the commencement of the difeafe, even before it has acquired a pus-like appearance; indeed I am not confident whether this property in the matter does not entirely ceafe as foon as it is fecreted in the form of pus. I am induced to think it does ceafe *, and that it is the thin darkifh-looking fluid only, oozing from the newly-formed cracks in the heels, fimilar to what fometimes appears from eryfipelatous blifters, which gives the difeafe. Nor am I certain that the nipples of the cows are at all times in a ftate to receive the infection. The appearance of the difeafe in the fpring and the

---

* It is very eafy to procure pus from old fores on the heels of horfes. This I have often inferted into fcratches made with a lancet, on the found nipples of cows, and have feen no other effects from it than fimple inflammation.

early

early part of the fummer, when they are difpofed to be affected with fpontaneous eruptions fo much more frequently than at other feafons, induces me to think, that the virus from the horfe muft be received upon them when they are in this ftate, in order to produce effects: experiments, however, muft determine thefe points. But it is clear that when the Cow-pox virus is once generated, that the cows cannot refift the contagion, in whatever ftate their nipples may chance to be, if they are milked with an infected hand.

Whether the matter, either from the cow or the horfe will affect the found fkin of the human body, I cannot pofitively determine; probably it will not, unlefs on thofe parts where the cuticle is extremely thin, as on the lips for example.

H   I have

I have known an inſtance of a poor girl who produced an ulceration on her lip by frequently holding her finger to her mouth to cool the raging of a Cow-pox ſore by blowing upon it. The hands of the farmers' ſervants here, from the nature of their employments, are conſtantly ex-poſed to thoſe injuries which occaſion abraſions of the cuticle, to punctures from thorns and ſuch like accidents; ſo that they are always in a ſtate to feel the conſequences of expoſure to infectious matter.

It is ſingular to obſerve that the Cow-pox virus, although it renders the conſtitution unſuſceptible of the variolous, ſhould, neverthelefs, leave it unchanged with reſpect to its own action. I have

already

already produced an inftance * to point out this, and fhall now corroborate it with another.

Elizabeth Wynne, who had the Cow-pox in the year 1759, was inoculated with variolous matter, without effect, in the year 1797, and again caught the Cow-pox in the year 1798. When I faw her, which was on the 8th day after fhe received the infection, I found her affected with general laffi-tude, fhiverings, alternating with heat, coldnefs of the extremities, and a quick and irregular pulfe. Thefe fymptoms were preceded by a pain in the axilla. On her hand was one large puftu-lous fore, which refembled that delinated in Plate No. 1.

* See Cafe IX.

H 2   It

It is curious alſo to obſerve, that the virus, which with reſpect to its effects is undetermined and uncertain previouſly to its paſſing from the horſe through the medium of the cow, ſhould then not only become more active, but ſhould invariably and completely poſſeſs thoſe ſpecific properties which induce in the human conſtitution ſymptoms ſimilar to thoſe of the variolous fever, and effect in it that peculiar change which for ever renders it unſuſceptible of the variolous contagion.

May it not, then, be reaſonably conjectured, that the ſource of the Small-pox is morbid matter of a peculiar kind, generated by a diſeaſe in the horſe, and that accidental circumſtances may have again and again ariſen, ſtill working new changes upon it, it, until it has acquired the contagious and malignant form under which we now commonly fee it making its devaftations amongft us? And, from a confideration of the change which the infectious matter undergoes from producing a difeafe on the cow, may we not conceive that many contagious difeafes, now prevalent among us, may owe their prefent appearance not to a fimple, but to a compound origin? For example, is it difficult to imagine that the meafles, the fcarlet fever, and the ulcerous fore throat with a fpotted fkin, have all fprung from the fame fource, affuming fome variety in their forms according to the nature of their new combinations? The fame queftion will apply refpecting the origin of many other contagious difeafes, which bear a ftrong analogy to each other.

There

There are certainly more forms than one,
without confidering the common variation between the confluent and diftinct, in which the
Small-pox appears in what is called the natural
way.—About feven years ago a fpecies of Small-
pox fpread through many of the towns and
villages of this part of Gloucefterfhire: it was
of fo mild a nature, that a fatal inftance was
fcarcely ever heard of, and confequently fo little
dreaded by the lower orders of the community,
that they fcrupled not to hold the fame intercourfe
with each other as if no infectious difeafe had been
prefent among them. I never faw nor heard of
an inftance of its being confluent. The moft
accurate manner, perhaps, in which I can convey
an idea of it is, by faying, that had fifty indi-
viduals been taken promifcuoufly and infected

by

by expofure to this contagion, they would have
had as mild and light a difeafe as if they had
been inoculated with variolous matter in the
ufual way. The harmlefs manner in which
it fhewed itfelf could not arife from any peculiarity either in the feafon or the weather, for I
watched its progrefs upwards of a year without
perceiving any variation in its general appearance.
I confider it then as a *variety* of the Small-
pox *.

In fome of the preceding cafes I have noticed
the attention that was paid to the ftate of the

* My friend Dr. Hicks, of Briftol, who during the prevalence of this diftemper was refident at Gloucefter, and Phyfician to the Hofpital there,
(where it was feen foon after its firft appearance in this country) had opportunities
of making numerous obfervations upon it, which it is his intention to communicate to the Public.

variolous

variolous matter previous to the experiment of inferting it into the arms of thofe who had gone through the Cow-pox. This I conceived to be of great importance in conducting thefe experiments, and were it always properly attended to by thofe who inoculate for the Small-pox, it might prevent much fubfequent mifchief and confufion. With the view of enforcing fo neceffary a precaution, I fhall take the liberty of digreffing fo far as to point out fome unpleafant facts, relative to mifmanagement in this particular, which have fallen under my own obfervation.

A Medical Gentleman (now no more), who for many years inoculated in this neighbourhood, frequently preferved the variolous matter intended for his ufe, on a piece of lint or cotton, which, in

its

its fluid ſtate was put into a vial, corked, and conveyed into a warm pocket; a ſituation certainly favourable for ſpeedily producing putrefaction in it. In this ſtate (not unfrequently after it had been taken ſeveral days from the puſtules) it was inſerted into the arms of his patients, and brought on inflammation of the inciſed parts, ſwellings of the axillary glands, fever, and ſometimes eruptions. But what was this diſeaſe? Certainly not the Small-pox; for the matter having from putrefaction loſt, or ſuffered a derangement in its ſpecific properties, was no longer capable of producing that malady, thoſe who had been inoculated in this manner being as much ſubject to the contagion of the Small-pox, as if they had never been under the influence of this artificial diſeaſe; and many, unfortunately, fell

I   victims

victims to it, who thought themselves in perfect security. The same unfortunate circumstance of giving a disease, supposed to be the Small-pox, with inefficaceous variolous matter, having occurred under the direction of some other practitioners within my knowledge, and probably from the same incautious method of securing the variolous matter, I avail myself of this opportunity of mentioning what I conceive to be of great importance; and, as a further cautionary hint, I shall again digress so far as to add another observation on the subject of Inoculation

Whether it be yet ascertained by experiment, that the quantity of variolous matter inserted into the skin makes any difference with respect to the subsequent mildness or violence of the disease, I

know

know not ; but I have the ftrongeft reafon for
fuppofing that if either the punctures or incifions
be made fo deep as to go *through* it, and wound
the adipofe membrane, that the rifk of bringing
on a violent difeafe is greatly increafed.   I have
known an inoculator, whofe practice was " to
cut deep enough (to ufe his own expreffion) to fee
a bit of fat," and there to lodge the matter.   The
great number of bad Cafes, independent of inflammations and abfceffes on the arms, and the fatality
which attended this practice was almoft incon-
ceivable ; and I cannot account for it on any
other principle than that of the matter being placed
in this fituation inftead of the fkin.

It was the practice of another, whom I well
remember, to pinch up a fmall portion of the fkin

on

on the arms of his patients and to pafs through it a needle, with a thread attached to it previoufly dipped in variolous matter. The thread was lodged in the perforated part, and confequently left in contact with the cellular membrane. This practice was attended with the fame ill fuccefs as the former. Although it is very improbable that any one would now inoculate in this rude way by defign, yet thefe obfervations may tend to place a double guard over the lancet, when infants, whofe fkins are comparatively fo very thin, fall under the care of the inoculator.

A very refpectable friend of mine, Dr. Hardwicke, of Sodbury in this county, inoculated great numbers of patients previous to the introduction of the more moderate method by Sutton, and with

fuch

fuch fuccefs, that a fatal inftance occurred as rarely as fince that method has been adopted. It was the doctor's practice to make as flight an incifion as poffible *upon* the fkin, and there to lodge a thread faturated with the variolous matter. When his patients became indifpofed, agreeably to the cuftom then prevailing, they were directed to go to bed and were kept moderately warm. Is it not probable then, that the fuccefs of the modern practice may depend more upon the method of invariably depofiting the virus in or upon the fkin, than on the fubfequent treatment of the difeafe?

I do not mean to infinuate that expofure to cool air, and fuffering the patient to drink cold water when hot and thirfty, may not moderate the eruptive fymptoms and leffen the number of puftules;

yet

yet, to repeat my former obſervation, I cannot
account for the uninterrupted ſuccefs, or nearly ſo,
of one practitioner, and the wretched ſtate of the
patients under the care of another, where, in both
inſtances, the general treatment did not differ
eſſentially, without conceiving it to ariſe from the
different modes of inſerting the matter for the
purpoſe of producing the diſeaſe. As it is not the
identical matter inſerted which is abſorbed into the
conſtitution, but that which is, by ſome peculiar
procefs in the animal economy, generated by it,
is it not probable that different parts of the human
body may prepare or modify the virus differently?
Although the ſkin, for example, adipoſe membrane, or mucous membranes are all capable of
producing the variolous virus by the ſtimulus given
by the particles originally depoſited upon them,

yet

yet I am induced to conceive that each of thefe parts is capable of producing fome variation in the qualities of the matter previous to its affecting the conftitution. What elfe can conftitute the difference between the Small-pox when communicated cafually or in what has been termed the natural way, or when brought on artificially through the medium of the fkin? After all, are the variolous particles, poffeffing their true fpecific and contagious principles, ever taken up and conveyed by the lymphatics unchanged into the blood veffels? I imagine not. Were this the cafe, fhould we not find the blood fufficiently loaded with them in fome ftages of the Small-pox to communicate the difeafe by inferting it under the cuticle, or by fpreading it on the furface of an ulcer? Yet experiments have determined the im-

practicability

practicability of its being given in this way; although it has been proved that variolous matter when much diluted with water, and applied to the fkin in the ufual manner, will produce the difeafe. But it would be digreffing beyond a proper boundary, to go minutely into this fubject here.

At what period the Cow-pox was firft noticed here is not upon record. Our oldeft farmers were not unacquainted with it in their earlieft days, when it appeared among their farms without any deviation from the phænomena which it now exhibits. Its connection with the Small-pox feems to have been unknown to them. Probably the general introduction of inoculation firft occafioned the difcovery.

Its

Its rife in this country may not have been of very remote date, as the practice of milking cows might formerly have been in the hands of women only; which I believe is the cafe now in fome other dairy countries, and, confequently that the cows might not in former times have been expofed to the contagious matter brought by the men fervants from the heels of horfes *. Indeed a knowledge of the fource of the infection is new in the minds of moft of the farmers in this neighbourhood, but it has at length produced good confequences; and it feems probable from the precautions they are now difpofed to adopt, that the

* I have been informed from refpectable authority that in Ireland, although dairies abound in many parts of the Ifland, the difeafe is entirely unknown. The reafon feems obvious. The bufinefs of the dairy is conducted by women only. Were the meaneft vaffal among the men, employed there as a milker at a dairy, he would feel his fituation unpleafant beyond all endurance.

K   appearance

appearance of the Cow-pox here may either be entirely extinguifhed or become extremely rare.

Should it be afked whether this inveftigation is a matter of mere curiofity, or whether it tends to any beneficial purpofe? I fhould anfwer, that notwithftanding the happy effects of Inoculation, with all the improvements which the practice has received fince its firft introduction into this country, it not very unfrequently produces deformity of the fkin, and fometimes, under the beft management, proves fatal.

Thefe circumftances muft naturally create in every inftance fome degree of painful folicitude for its confequences. But as I have never known fatal effects arife from the Cow-pox, even when impreffed

impreffed in the moft unfavourable manner, producing extenfive inflammations and fuppurations
on the hands; and as it clearly appears that this
difeafe leaves the conftitution in a ftate of perfect
fecurity from the infection of the Small-pox, may
we not infer that a mode of Inoculation may be
introduced preferable to that at prefent adopted,
efpecially among thofe families, which, from
previous circumftances we may judge to be predifpofed to have the difeafe unfavourably? It is an
excefs in the number of puftules which we chiefly
dread in the Small-pox; but, in the Cow-pox, no
puftules appear, nor does it feem poffible for the
contagious matter to produce the difeafe from
effluvia, or by any other means than contact, and
that probably not fimply between the virus and
the cuticle; fo that a fingle individual in a family

might

might at any time receive it without the rifk of infecting the reft, or of fpreading a diftemper that fills a country with terror. Several inftances have come under my obfervation which juftify the affertion that the difeafe cannot be propagated by effluvia. The firft boy whom I inoculated with the matter of Cow-pox, flept in a bed, while the experiment was going forward, with two children who never had gone through either that difeafe or the Small-pox, without infecting either of them.

A young woman who had the Cow-pox to a great extent, feveral fores which maturated having appeared on the hands and wrifts, flept in the fame bed with a fellow-dairy maid who never had been infected with either the Cow-pox or the Small-pox, but no indifpofition followed.

Another

Another inftance has occurred of a young woman on whofe hands were feveral large fuppurations from the Cow-pox, who was at the fame time a daily nurfe to an infant, but the complaint was not communicated to the child.

In fome other points of view, the inoculation of this difeafe appears preferable to the variolous inoculation.

In conftitutions predifpofed to fcrophula, how frequently we fee the inoculated Small-pox, roufe into activity that diftrefsful malady. This circumftance does not feem to depend on the manner in which the diftemper has fhewn itfelf, for it has as frequently happened among thofe who have had it mildly, as when it has appeared in the contrary way.

There

There are many, who from fome peculiarity in the habit refift the common effects of variolous matter inferted into the fkin, and who are in confequence haunted through life with the diftreffing idea of being infecure from fubfequent infection. A ready mode of diffipating anxiety originating from fuch a caufe muft now appear obvious. And, as we have feen that the conftitution may at any time be made to feel the febrile attack of Cowpox, might it not, in many chronic difeafes be introduced into the fyftem, with the probability of affording relief, upon well-known phyfiological principles?

Although I fay the fyftem may at any time be made to feel the febrile attack of Cow-pox, yet I have a fingle inftance before me where the virus

acted

acted locally only, but it is not in the least probable that the fame perfon would refift the action
both of the Cow-pox virus and the variolous.

Elizabeth Sarfenet lived as a dairy maid at New-
park farm, in this parifh. All the cows and the fervants employed in milking had the Cow-pox; but
this woman, though fhe had feveral fores upon
her fingers, felt no tumors in the axillæ, nor any
general indifpofition. On being afterwards cafually expofed to variolous infection, fhe had the
Small-pox in a mild way.—Hannah Pick, another
of the dairy maids who was a fellow-fervant with
Elizabeth Sarfenet when the diftemper broke out
at the farm was, at the fame time infected; but
this young woman had not only fores upon her
hands, but felt herfelf alfo much indifpofed for a

day

day or two. After this, I made feveral attempts to give her the Small-pox by inoculation, but they all proved fruitlefs. From the former Cafe then we fee that the animal economy is fubject to the fame laws in one difeafe as the other.

The following Cafe which has very lately occurred renders it highly probable that not only the heels of the horfe, but other parts of the body of that animal, are capable of generating the virus which produces the Cow-pox.

An extenfive inflammation of the eryfipelatous kind, appeared without any apparent caufe upon the upper part of the thigh of a fucking colt, the property of Mr. Millet, a farmer at Rockhampton, a village near Berkeley. The inflammation continued

tinued feveral weeks, and at length terminated in the formation of three or four fmall abfceffes. The inflamed parts were fomented, and dreffings were applied by fome of the fame perfons who were employed in milking the cows. The number of cows milked was twenty-four, and the whole of them had the Cow-pox. The milkers, confifting of the farmer's wife, a man and a maid fervant, were infected by the cows. The man fervant had previoufly gone through the Small-pox, and felt but little of the Cow-pox. The fervant maid had fome years before been infected with the Cow-pox, and fhe alfo felt it now in a flight degree: But the farmer's wife who never had gone through either of thefe difeafes, felt its effects very feverely.

L   That

That the difeafe produced upon the cows by the colt and from thence conveyed to thofe who milked them was the *true* and not the *fpurious* Cow-pox*, there can be fcarcely any room for fufpicion; yet it would have been more completely fatisfactory, had the effects of variolous matter been afcertained on the farmer's wife, but there was a peculiarity in her fituation which prevented my making the experiment.

Thus far have I proceeded in an inquiry, founded, as it muft appear, on the bafis of ex-periment; in which, however, conjecture has been occafionally admitted in order to prefent to perfons well fituated for fuch difcuffions, objects

* See Note in Page 7.

for

for a more minute inveſtigation.   In the mean
time I ſhall myſelf continue to proſecute this
inquiry, encouraged by the hope of its becoming
eſſentially beneficial to mankind.

FINIS.

ERRATA.

Page 5, Line 4, after the word *shiverings* insert *succeeded by heat.*
Line 16, for *needlessly* read *heedlessly.*

—— 24, Last line but one, for *sore* read *tumour.*

—— 40, Line 12, for *Macklove* read *Marklove.*

—— 41, Note—for *scepticus* read *septicus.*

—— 60, Last line, for *moderate* read *modern.*

This special edition of

AN INQUIRY

INTO THE CAUSES AND EFFECTS OF

THE VARIOLÆ VACCINÆ

has been privately printed for the members of
The Classics of Medicine Library by lithog-
raphy at The Meriden Gravure Co. Film was
prepared from an original 1798 edition fur-
nished to the publisher courtesy The Francis A.
Countway Library of Medicine. New type
matter was composed by the Press of A. Colish,
Inc. in Monotype Baskerville. The text paper
is Curtis Rag natural. The volume has been
bound in top grain cowhide with endleaves in
a marbled design by Tapley-Rutter, Inc.,
Bookbinders. Edges are gilded, and covers are
brass-die stamped in 22-karat gold. Cover
stampings, design and production of the edition
by Max M. Stein.

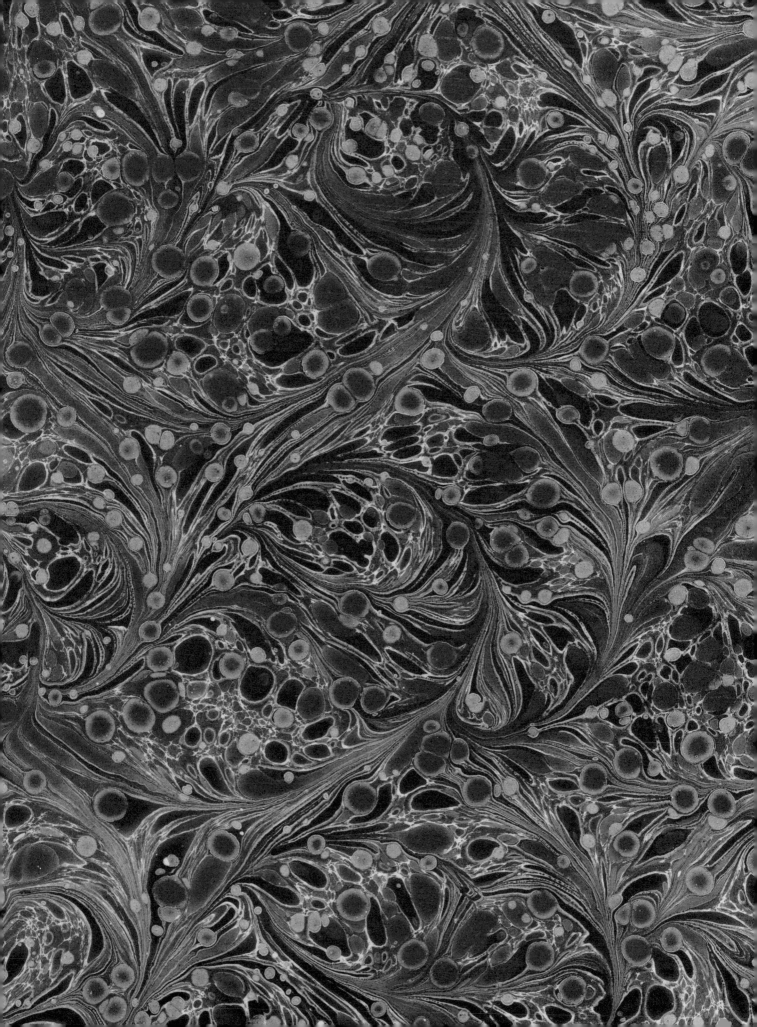